Another Glorious Year

Another Glorious Year

Sarah ShaBazz

CONTENTS

Library of Congress Control Number: 2026911224

First Printing, 2026

For the teachers who taught us,
the friends who grew with us,
and the little girl in me who believed one day she would do something great.

1

The Early Years of Glorious

I did not begin my journey at Glorious Baptist Day School in kindergarten like many of the other children.

I arrived in second grade.

But even before school officially started, I attended a two-week summer program that helped me learn the rhythm of Glorious before becoming a full-time student.

Those two weeks felt magical.

We went on field trips that seemed bigger than life itself. We visited Sea World, Knott's Berry Farm, Universal Studios, and other places that, to a child from South Central Los Angeles, felt like entire new worlds. Riding the bus with classmates, singing songs, and eating packed lunches made me feel like I already belonged somewhere special.

Our teacher was Miss Patterson.

She was young, newly out of college, and the niece of the church and school's owner. Music seemed to live inside her. She talked about working around the group The Fifth Dimension, the singers of "Aquarius." Whether she had actually worked with them or had simply been in their circle, we believed every word because she carried herself like someone connected to real music and real stages.

Under Miss Patterson, we sang all the time.

We even appeared on Channel 68 several times, performing with other private schools. I remember it feeling a little like a competition, although to us it mostly just felt exciting to be on television. Singing together made us proud. We stood a little taller when we wore our matching outfits.

One afternoon, about two days before a performance, my mother found a pattern and a swatch of fabric stuffed deep inside my book bag. It was the notice for the outfit we were supposed to wear. She was upset that I had not shown it to her sooner. There was barely any time left. But my mother did what mothers do. Somehow, she made it happen. When the day came, I stood there dressed just like everyone else, grateful that she had pulled it off.

In that class was a girl named Valerie.

She was brilliant, the kind of student teachers quietly watched with amazement. After second grade, she skipped third grade entirely and moved straight into fourth. We also attended church together, and even after she advanced, she still remained connected to our class in some ways. During spelling tests, she hardly needed to participate because she already knew every word. To us, she seemed almost grown.

Miss Patterson believed learning should prepare us for real life, not just schoolwork.

One of the most memorable things she taught us was telephone etiquette.

She set up real telephones in the classroom so we could practice speaking properly. One phone would ring, and one student would answer while another responded from across the room. We learned how to greet someone politely, how to ask for a person respectfully, and how to speak clearly so we could be understood.

"Hello, may I please speak to..."

"This is she speaking."

"Please hold."

We practiced until our voices sounded confident and sure. It felt very grown up, as though we were being trusted with the world of adults.

She also introduced us to French.

At seven years old, I did not realize how special that was. I still remember the little song she taught us, "Moi, j'aime..." about loving our dog, our cat, our mother, and our father. We sang it again and again until the words stayed with me long after second grade ended. Long after I forgot worksheets and spelling lists, I still remembered how to say what I loved in another language.

Miss son even taught us how to crochet.

My mother bought me a tiny crochet needle and yarn that looked like pieces of cut string and told me I was going to make a doily. I remember feeling confused because I thought she meant a doll. Still, I learned. My small hands moved awkwardly at first, looping and pulling, trying to understand the rhythm of the thread. But slowly, something clicked.

At seven years old, my hands discovered a skill that would stay with me for the rest of my life.

Years later, when I became a mother myself, I crocheted blankets for my babies. Soft, careful stitches made with patience I did not know I had back then. I never realized at the time that a second-grade classroom had quietly given me something I would carry into adulthood.

That same year, there was an audition announcement for a show.

Someone explained that they were looking for a small, petite girl to jump up and down and deliver a line. I was not asked to audition. They were looking for a petite, light-skinned girl, and that description did not include me. At the time, I did not fully understand what that meant. I only knew that I watched from the sidelines while others were considered.

By third grade, my teacher was Mrs. Byrd .

That was the year friendships deepened.

I became especially close to KiKi and Monique. KiKi rode the bus every day from Culver City, which felt very far from our neighborhood. She arrived just in time for school and left immediately afterward, so our time together was limited to the classroom.

Monique was different. She stayed for extended day just like I did. We were there early in the mornings and late into the evenings, sharing long hours that turned classmates into real friends. We did homework together, played together, and learned how to exist in that in-between space where school felt almost like a second home.

During that year, something unusual happened.

Our school became part of a movie called The Bus Is Coming.

A film crew arrived and used our campus while we played outside as usual. We slid down the slide, spun on the merry-go-round, and climbed the jungle gym while cameras quietly captured the background of childhood.

Later, my mother went to see the movie and came home excited. She said she spotted either me or my sister going down the slide. She knew because that day, instead of wearing our forest green V-neck sweaters with the school logo, she had bought us bright pink cardigan sweaters. They stood out so clearly that she recognized us immediately. I am still surprised we were allowed to wear them, but since we were outside, the rules about outerwear must have been more relaxed.

Fourth grade brought Miss John.

She was the first, and only, White teacher I remember seeing at Glorious. I thought she was very tall, although at eight years old everyone seemed tall. She wore either a red gingham dress or a blue gingham dress every single day. She called them her uniforms, and I never saw her wear anything else.

I do not remember as many details from that year, but one lesson stayed with me.

One day I said the vegetable okra the way I had always heard it spoken, sounding more like "oakry." Miss John gently corrected me.

"It is pronounced okra," she said.

It was a small moment, but it opened my ears to language, to the idea that words could sound different depending on where you were and who was teaching you. At Glorious, learning did not come only from books. It came from people, corrections, friendships, music, and moments that slowly shaped who I was becoming.

By the time fifth grade arrived, Glorious no longer felt new.

It felt like mine.

And by then, without even realizing it, I had already begun collecting the memories that would stay with me for the rest of my life.

2

Back to School

Summer was over, and it was time for us to go back to Glorious Baptist Day School.

When school started that fall, everything felt a little different. We were in sixth grade now. That meant we were the oldest students in the school, the top class, the ones everybody else looked up to. After all those years of watching the older children, it was finally our turn. Sixth grade. We had made it.

There were only ten of us in my grade now, and this year we shared our classroom with the fifth graders, who numbered about twelve. One familiar face was there too, although in a different way. Camille was in fifth grade again. Mrs. Grace said she needed to work with her a little more so she could have a solid foundation. Camille was small for her age, and somehow it did not seem strange for her to be with the younger group. We all just treated her like one of the fifth graders, and Camille seemed perfectly comfortable with that.

At the beginning of the school year, though, one person was missing.

Lynn was not there.

She had gone to spend the summer with her grandmother in Idaho, and she was not coming back for another month. Her absence left a space in the room that all of us could feel, even if nobody said it out loud.

Back then, I would have called Lynn the ring leader.

She was the tallest girl in the class, and in many ways, she was the boss. The rest of us usually went along with whatever Lynn thought, said, or decided. She seemed to know more than the rest of us about things outside our little private school world. Lynn had cousins who went to the local public school, and through them she learned all kinds of things that seemed new and exciting to us. Whatever she heard, whatever she found out, whatever was going on beyond Glorious Baptist Day School, Lynn brought it back and shared it with the rest of us. Because of that, we listened to her.

Without Lynn there, the room felt a little quieter and a little less certain.

Not long after school started, Mrs. Grace pulled me aside.

"Denise," she said, "you are a leader, and it is about time you started acting like a leader and stopped being a follower."

Those words settled deep inside me.

I had never thought of myself that way before. I was not loud. I was not pushy. I was not the kind of person who tried to take over a room. But Mrs. Grace saw something in me, and when Mrs. Grace spoke that way, I listened.

So I tried.

With Lynn away, I stepped into the space that had been left open. I became a soft-spoken leader. I did not lead by being bossy or demanding. I led quietly, with calm words and steady ways. It was different from Lynn's style, but it worked. For that short season, I carried myself a little taller. I began to see that leadership did not always have to be loud to be real.

Then, when Lynn returned a month later, I let her slip back into her old role without a fight. That was just how things had always been. Still, something had changed. I had heard Mrs. Grace's words, and I could not unhear them. Somewhere inside, I now knew I had the makings of a leader too.

This year already felt like it was going to be special.

We were not the little children anymore. We were no longer looking up at the older students and wondering what it would feel like to be in their place. Now we were the ones at the top. The ones with the biggest desks, the hardest work, the most responsibility, and the greatest privilege.

We were sixth graders now.

We were the top dogs in the school.

And I had a feeling this was going to be another glorious year.

3

The New Fishbowl

At the beginning of sixth grade, Mrs. Grace gifted our class a brand-new fishbowl. We were all excited the moment we saw it. It was nothing like the plain bowls people usually kept fish in. This one was crystal, and it sat on top of a brass pedestal. When it turned, it played the song "How Dry I Am." The whole thing seemed fancy and beautiful to us, and none of us had ever seen anything like it before.

Finley and Goldie seemed to like it too.

Of course, like everything else in our classroom, taking care of the fishbowl became one of our shared responsibilities. We took turns cleaning it. When it was time, we would scoop Finley and Goldie out with a little fishnet and place them carefully into a peanut butter jar while we carried the bowl to the restroom to wash it out and fill it with fresh water.

I was known for being clumsy. It seemed like I always had a skinned knee. If it was not freshly scraped, it had a scab on it. That was just how I was.

One day, it was my turn to clean the fishbowl.

I carefully carried the crystal bowl into the girls' restroom. I poured the old water out, washed the bowl, and filled it with fresh water. I was trying to be extra careful because I knew how special it was. But when I turned around to head back to the classroom, the bowl slipped from my hands.

It crashed to the floor.

Crystal glass shattered everywhere.

I just stood there for a moment, staring at the mess. Then I grabbed paper towels and cleaned it up as best I could. When I finished, I walked back to the classroom without the bowl.

Mrs. Grace took one look at me and already knew what had happened.

I apologized, and she told me it was okay.

But I did not think it was really okay.

That beautiful crystal fishbowl was gone, and I knew there would not be another one like it.

The next fish home we got was just a plain, regular, triangle-shaped aquarium. It was probably the nicest and biggest place Finley and Goldie ever had to live. It came with little rocks, water plants, and even a filter. It was a real aquarium, practical and sturdy, and it did the job well.

Still, it was not the crystal bowl.

And after that day, no one ever mentioned the crystal fishbowl again.

4

Meeting Family

After the fishbowl catastrophe, Mrs. Grace was a little more careful about what she allowed me to do. I could not really blame her. Dropping that beautiful crystal fishbowl had not exactly helped my reputation.

One day, Mrs. Grace's sisters came to visit our classroom. They brought their children with them because they were on their way to Disneyland. That alone was exciting enough, but what really caught my attention was the newborn baby one of them was carrying.

I loved babies.

I always had.

The moment I saw that tiny baby, I wanted to hold him. I asked Mrs. Grace if I could, and she gave me a look that said everything without her having to say a word. It was the kind of look that clearly meant, I remember what you did to that fishbowl, and I do not want you dropping my nephew.

I was crushed.

I knew exactly why she looked at me that way, but it still hurt my feelings. I was clumsy, yes, but this was a baby, and I loved babies. I would have been so careful.

After a while, Mrs. Grace must have decided to give me a chance. She allowed me to sit down and hold the baby, but only for about a minute. I was happy just to have that much. I sat very still, holding him as carefully as I could, trying to enjoy every second before he was taken back.

Soon her sister picked the baby up, and before long they were on their way again.

By then, we had already met several members of Mrs. Grace's family. We knew her husband, Andrew, her son, Andrew Junior, and her daughter, Daisy. Now we were meeting her sisters too. Their names were Faith and Hope, which seemed fitting somehow. I always thought those were beautiful names.

What I remember most was that the girls in the family all seemed to have flower names. Mrs. Grace's daughter was Daisy, and her nieces were Lily, Gardenia, and Rose. I thought that was the prettiest thing. It made their family seem even more special to me, like they belonged in a storybook.

Mrs. Grace had a beautiful family, and getting little glimpses of them made me feel like I knew her even better. Teachers often seemed like they belonged only at school, as if they stepped into the classroom each morning just to teach us and then disappeared when the day was over. But moments like that reminded me that Mrs. Grace had a whole life and a whole family beyond our classroom.

And for one brief minute, I got to hold a tiny piece of it in my arms.

5

The New Student

One day after lunch, a new student walked quietly into our classroom.

She stood near the door holding her book bag, looking a little unsure of herself. I noticed her right away. She was tall, taller than me but not quite as tall as Lynn. She had on the uniform blouse, the white one with the Peter Pan collar, but instead of the regular uniform skirt, she was wearing a plaid skirt that was a little different. She was very fair-skinned, with light brown hair that was almost blonde.

I turned around to look at her more closely, and then I recognized her.

It was Juanita from third grade.

As soon as I realized who she was, I got excited. Juanita and I already knew each other from years before. Her sister Renee had been in the same class as my sister Yvette, and they had been friends since first grade. Once I recognized Juanita, she began to remember us too. She was not really a stranger after all. She was someone coming back into our world.

That made it easier for both of us.

I spent a lot of time with Juanita after that. In the mornings before school started, we would be together, and one of the things I remember most is walking her little brother Tommy down the street to preschool. Tommy was only three years old. Juanita and I would each hold one of his hands and walk him carefully down the sidewalk to the preschool a block away from the day school we attended.

I can still picture it.

The three of us walking together, Tommy in the middle, his little hands stretched up to reach ours.

There was something sweet about that routine. It made us feel older and responsible, like we were helping take care of something important. We were already the oldest students in the school, and moments like that reminded me that sixth grade came with a different kind of feeling. We were still children, but we were growing up too.

Juanita's arrival changed the rhythm of the class a little. She was not just a new student. To me, she was someone familiar, someone connected to people I already knew, someone who fit into the story of our school even before she officially stepped back into it.

By the time the day was over, she did not feel new anymore.

She felt like she belonged.

6

Runaway Student

By the time I was in sixth grade, I had already been given real responsibilities around the school. One of them was helping with the kindergartners. I would walk them to the kindergarten room and stay with them until their teacher was ready to begin. Looking back on it now, I can see that I was in training to become a teacher and did not even know it yet. At the time, I was just an older student helping out. Years later, I would realize I was already learning how to guide children, keep them busy, explain things, and step in when needed.

Sometimes I was also called into the kindergarten class to interpret.

No, the children did not speak Spanish or any language other than English. They just spoke kindergarten. Sometimes the teacher could not understand what one of them was trying to say, and she would call me in to explain. Somehow, I could usually figure it out.

When I stayed with the kindergartners, sometimes I read them stories, and sometimes I played games with them. One day, I decided to teach them Heads Down, Thumbs Up, Seven Up. I thought it was a great idea. I was sure they would enjoy it.

It did not work out the way I expected.

I had the children put their heads down and stick their thumbs up the way you were supposed to. Then one child would walk around and press somebody's thumb, and the person who was chosen was supposed to keep their head down, put their thumb in, and later guess who had touched them.

That was the plan.

But one little boy clearly did not understand the game at all. He sat there with his head down and his thumb up, just like he was told. Then, whenever another child pinched his thumb, he would pop his head up and hit the student next to him. He thought the child beside him was hurting him on purpose. He did not realize that getting his thumb touched was the whole point of the game. He was supposed to put his thumb down and later guess who had touched him, not come up swinging at the nearest child.

It took a while before I realized he did not understand the game.

Once I figured it out, I could not help but laugh. I had tried to bring a fun sixth-grade game into kindergarten, and instead I had chaos. That should have told me that not every game works with every age group.

Then one day, the kindergarten teacher came in frantic.

A little girl had run away from the kindergarten classroom.

She had asked to go to the restroom, but she never came back. When the teacher went to check on her, she was not there. At first, everyone searched the school. They looked in every classroom, every hallway, and every possible corner. When they still could not find her, the adults and even some of the older students went out into the neighborhood to look.

The sixth-grade students were sent to help search for the missing child, along with the kindergarten teacher and our sixth-grade teacher.

I did not go out looking for her.

Instead, I was sent to the kindergarten classroom to stay with the rest of the children until their teacher returned. That became my part in the group effort. I stayed with the kindergartners, keeping them calm and occupied while everyone else searched.

Even then, without realizing it, I was doing teacher work.

I do not remember every detail of that hour, but I do remember the feeling. The whole school was unsettled. Even though I was not outside searching, I knew something serious was happening. We all did.

It was probably about an hour before they found her.

The restrooms were behind the classroom area, just outside the door and to the left. Somehow, instead of going back to class, the little girl had walked around to the front of the school and gone right out of the front gate. She had made her way five blocks to her father's house.

Apparently, her parents had separated, and she wanted to see her dad.

That was where they found her, safe at his house. Later, she was brought back to school.

I was relieved when I heard she was okay.

At the time, it felt like such a big event, and in truth, it was. A little kindergartner had left the school grounds and walked through the neighborhood by herself. It took all of us, in different ways, to help that day. Some searched the streets, some checked the school, and I stayed behind to watch the little ones who were left in the classroom.

That was my assignment.

And in its own way, it mattered too.

And maybe that was part of how my journey to becoming a teacher had already begun, long before I ever knew it myself.

7

Raindrops Keep Falling on My Head

May Day was coming up again, and that always meant something special was being planned.

That year, we had custom costumes made by one of the parents. The girls' outfits were beautiful. Each one had a skirt with ruffles and a halter top. We were paired with partners, and each pair wore the same pastel color. There was light blue, pink, lime green, yellow, and lavender.

I was assigned lavender.

The boys wore white shirts, white pants, and sashes in one of the pastel colors. They also wore sombreros, which made the whole performance look even more festive. Our class danced to "Raindrops Keep Fallin' on My Head," and along with our pastel costumes, the girls carried parasols as part of the routine.

To get ready for the big day, we had to make the umbrellas ourselves.

One day, one of the parents came in with twelve wire umbrellas. That became our art project. First, we had to wrap every part of the wire with white cloth tape. We had to cover each section carefully so no bare wire would show. After that, we were given strips of tulle to finish decorating them.

My umbrella was lavender, just like my dress.

I remember being proud of it because it matched perfectly. It felt special carrying something that had been made just for our performance and decorated in my color.

My sister did not get one that year because the parent only made outfits for the girls who were actually in the performance. I knew she probably would have enjoyed having one too, but this time the costumes and umbrellas were just for us.

When May Day finally arrived, it went off very well, just as it usually did.

The second graders braided the Maypole, and the whole day was filled with food, laughter, and fun. It was one of those school traditions that everybody looked forward to. There was always a feeling of excitement in the air, with children dressed up, families gathered around, and everyone enjoying the celebration together.

We did not have anyone from our class in the Queen's Court that year, so all of us participated in the performance.

That was just fine with me.

I was happy to be out there in my lavender costume, holding my lavender parasol, dancing with my classmates to "Raindrops Keep Fallin' on My Head." It felt pretty and polished and important, the kind of school memory that stays with you because everything came together just right.

And like so many things at Glorious, it was not just a program.

It was an event.

It was a celebration.

It was another part of a glorious year.

8

Too Close for Comfort

By sixth grade, I had started paying more attention to the world outside our neighborhood.

The year before, during fifth grade, there had been a day when the world outside our little school suddenly felt very close.

We were sitting in class when we heard helicopters overhead.

Not one.

Several.

They circled and circled loudly enough to make us look up from our papers. Then police cars raced past the school with sirens blaring and lights flashing. The sound bounced against the buildings and pushed through the classroom windows.

For a few moments, none of us knew what was happening.

Glorious Baptist Day School usually felt tucked away from the rest of Los Angeles. Inside our classroom, we had spelling words, math problems, recorder practice, and Mrs. Grace. But that day, something serious was happening beyond the schoolyard.

Later, the grown-ups talked about it.

The news was full of reports about Patty Hearst, the young woman who had been kidnapped by a group called the Symbionese Liberation Army. At the time, I did not understand all the details. I only knew that adults were worried, television stations kept interrupting regular programs, and the helicopters seemed to stay in the sky forever.

Someone said the police were searching near a neighborhood not far from where our school was.

That made everything feel different.

The story was no longer just something on the evening news. It felt close enough to hear.

Still, inside our classroom, Mrs. Grace kept us steady. She did not let panic take over the room. She reminded us to keep working, to listen, and to stay calm.

That afternoon, when my mother picked us up from school, she decided to try driving toward the area everyone was talking about on the news. Like many people in Los Angeles, she was curious and wanted to see what all the commotion was about for herself.

But as we got closer, the roads were blocked off.

Police officers stood in the streets directing traffic while patrol cars forced drivers to turn around. Every route toward the neighborhood seemed closed. Cars were being detoured in every direction, and there was no way for us to get close enough to see anything ourselves.

I remember sitting in the car watching the flashing lights in the distance and realizing, maybe for the first time, that the frightening things adults talked about on television did not only happen far away.

Sometimes they happened close enough for helicopters to shake the sky above your school.

That was one of the things I remember most about Mrs. Grace.

Even when the outside world grew loud, she knew how to make the classroom feel safe.

9

Save the Best for Last

Some of my favorite memories from Glorious Baptist Day School happened outside at playtime.

We had all kinds of games we liked to play. One of my favorites was when the boys chased the girls and the girls chased the boys. The rules seemed to change depending on the day. Sometimes, if you got caught, you just had to sit on the bench until the game was over. Other times, if someone caught you, you had to sit next to that person and have lunch with them.

I did not run very fast, and I was easy to catch. But for a while, that did not really matter because nobody seemed very interested in catching me anyway, and I was perfectly fine with that.

Then there was Ray.

Ray always seemed to catch me and almost never anybody else. I never knew whether it was because I was slow and easy to catch or because he had a crush on me. I suspected it might have been both. I liked Ray just fine as a friend, almost like a brother, but there was nothing romantic there for me.

Sometimes we played softball or kickball. Every now and then, there might be another organized game too. No matter what we played, though, I was almost always chosen last. Two students would be team captains, and they would pick players one by one. Everybody knew I was not bringing many points to the team.

I was considered sorry.

After a while, I started joking about it myself. At the end of every selection process, when I was the last one standing, I would say, "I see you saved the best for last."

Everybody would laugh, because I was definitely not the best.

When we played kickball or softball, the ball never seemed to go more than about three feet when I hit it. Most of the time, I struck out. On the rare occasion that I made it to first base, usually because I had walked, I almost always got put out trying to run to second. Even if the person behind me hit well and the rest of the team started moving around the bases, somehow I would still be the one to get out before I could make it any farther.

The outfielders knew not to worry when it was my turn at bat. Sometimes they would actually sit down in the field because they already knew the ball was not coming anywhere near them. They treated my turn like a chance to rest.

That was just how it was.

There was no improving.

Part of the problem was that I had to be careful when I ran because I did not want to fall. Being careful made me even slower, and being slower made me even less successful at sports. It was a cycle that never really worked in my favor.

One time, we went on a field trip to a huge park. Several other private schools were there that day too. One of the activities at the park was a rope swing that people could grab and use to swing across a pit to the other side. There was always a long line for it, and the children seemed to love it.

I never even tried.

I already knew myself well enough to know that I was not capable of holding onto that rope and swinging across that pit. Some things were simply not for me, and that was one of them.

At that same park, they organized races for us to do, including a potato sack race and a three-legged race. I had no interest in racing at all. I already knew I was not going to win, and I did not see the point in proving it in public.

But then I got paired with Monique.

I agreed to do the three-legged race because if I did not, she would not have had a partner. So I let them tie our legs together. We were told to start on our common leg and work together. As soon as the whistle blew, we took off as fast as we could.

To my surprise, I was keeping up with her.

Not only that, we were doing really well.

Before I knew it, we had won.

I could hardly believe it. That was probably my first sports win ever. Monique and I had done a great job together, and for one shining moment, I knew what it felt like to come in first.

Unfortunately, that victory was short-lived.

It did not earn me any lasting credit for future athletic performances. I was still the same Denise everybody expected to be picked last. The students still teased me about being sorry in sports, and I just took it in stride.

I told them, "It is okay. One day I am going to do something great."

And deep down, I knew I would.

It would not be sports.

But it would be something great.

10

The White Cadillac

I remember Mrs. Grace's gold Cadillac Coupe de Ville. That car had become part of her presence at school. It seemed to match her style perfectly. But this was a new year, and now she had a new car.

This time it was a white Cadillac Coupe de Ville, trimmed in gold.

It was just as impressive as the gold one, maybe even more so. Mrs. Grace always seemed to have a way of carrying herself with elegance, and that white Cadillac fit right in with the picture of who she was in my mind.

We continued our tradition of walking Mrs. Grace to her car after school each day. It was a small procession of children carrying boxes, bags, books, or whatever else she needed taken out to the car. We were always glad to help. It felt important, almost ceremonial, like part of the rhythm of the school day.

One rainy afternoon, Louis had an idea.

He told Mrs. Grace, "Since it is raining, you can just give me the keys, and I will take your things to your car for you. That way, everyone does not have to get wet."

It sounded helpful enough, and Mrs. Grace handed him the keys.

A few minutes later, she headed out to her car with me and Juanita walking behind her. When we stepped out of the school gate, there it was.

Her white Cadillac was parked right in front of us, with the windshield wipers going and the lights on.

Louis jumped out of the car and ran up to her, beaming with pride.

He looked so pleased with himself, as if he had done something clever and useful.

But Mrs. Grace was not happy.

She lit into him immediately.

"Why would you drive my car?" she demanded. "That is much too dangerous! Anything could have happened."

Louis's smile disappeared.

"I was only trying to help," he said in his defense. "I did not want you to get wet."

I could tell he had not meant any harm. In his mind, he had probably done something thoughtful and grown-up. He had seen a problem and believed he had solved it.

After a moment, Mrs. Grace apologized for getting upset with him. She told him she knew he was only trying to help. Then she explained why it was so dangerous for him to drive her car in the rain as a twelve-year-old boy without a driver's license.

That made sense, of course.

Still, I remember the whole moment so clearly. The sight of that big white Cadillac sitting there with the wipers swishing, the headlights on, and Louis standing proudly beside it as though he had done Mrs. Grace the greatest favor in the world. Then, just as quickly, the shift when he realized that what he thought was helpful had actually been a very bad idea.

It was one of those school moments that was serious, but still unforgettable.

And like so many memories from Glorious Baptist Day School, it has stayed with me all these years later, clear as rain on a white Cadillac.

11

A New Word

We had a lot of fun in Mrs. Grace's class.

She believed in teaching us every chance she got, and her lessons did not stop with textbooks. Of course, we learned the regular school subjects. We had to stand in front of the class and recite poetry by famous poets like Robert Frost. I especially remember reciting "The Road Not Taken." We also had to recite our multiplication facts, and we had weekly spelling bees. Mrs. Lewis kept us on our toes. She wanted us to speak well, think carefully, and know our lessons.

But along with all the formal learning, there was always something alive in her classroom. We laughed there. We paid attention there. We learned from books, from each other, and sometimes from whatever happened to be going on right outside the window.

One afternoon, we were working quietly when someone pointed toward the classroom window.

Outside, a man was walking along the sidewalk near the black iron fence.

He staggered.

He leaned to one side, then to the other.

Even from inside the classroom, it was obvious that something was not right.

Mrs. Grace noticed us staring.

"All right," she said, folding her arms. "Tell me what you observe."

"He is drunk," someone said.

"He is intoxicated," another voice added.

Mrs. Grace nodded.

"Yes," she said. "Those are both correct."

Then she smiled a little.

"But there is another word that means the same thing."

We waited.

"In-e-bri-a-ted," she said slowly, writing it on the board.

Inebriated.

"It means impaired by alcohol," she explained. "Different word, same meaning."

We repeated it together.

"In-e-bri-a-ted."

Mrs. Grace clapped her hands once.

"See," she said, "life gives us lessons every day. You just have to pay attention."

That was the kind of teacher she was. She could take an unexpected moment and turn it into a vocabulary lesson before we even realized what she was doing.

After that, whenever we learned a new word, somebody would whisper, "Like inebriated," and the rest of us would smile.

Mrs. Grace knew how to teach, but she also knew how to laugh.

Sometimes our classroom antics caught her off guard, and even when she tried to be serious, we could still bring out her sense of humor.

One day, Donnell said something that shocked her.

He looked at Mrs. Grace and said, "You use LSD."

She was appalled.

She looked at him in disbelief and immediately told him that he was being rude and should never say anything like that again. Donnell, of course, was amused by her reaction.

He chuckled and said, "LSD. You use it every day."

That only made her more upset.

"Donnell," she said, "did they not tell you not to say that?"

"But you do," he insisted.

By then, she was growing more and more frustrated, and all of us were trying to figure out what in the world he meant.

Then he asked, "Do you not use lotion, soap, and deodorant?"

For a moment, the room was quiet.

Then Mrs. Grace broke into a smile, and the whole class exploded with laughter.

Even she had to laugh.

She gave Donnell a playful little punch on the shoulder and said, "Boy, you are something else."

That was Mrs. Grace's class.

We learned poetry and multiplication facts. We had spelling bees and vocabulary lessons. We were expected to stand up, speak clearly, and know our work. But mixed in with all of that were moments of laughter, surprise, and quick little lessons pulled from everyday life.

Mrs. Grace took every opportunity to teach us.

I was a very well-behaved child, but one day I said something that painted me into a corner.

Mrs. Grace told me that if I did not finish a task, I would not get a Big Stick popsicle. It was the first time she had ever brought Big Sticks. I knew what they were because I had seen people buy them from the ice cream truck, but I had never actually had one. In my mind, I preferred an orange Push-Up or an ice cream sandwich.

So when she threatened to withhold it, I quickly answered, "I do not like that anyway."

That was the problem.

From then on, every time Mrs. Grace brought Big Sticks, I felt like I had to keep saying I did not like them because I had said it that first time. I could not back down now. I had a reputation to protect, even if it was only with myself.

As it turned out, the next time my mother bought ice cream from the ice cream truck, I decided to try one.

I asked for a Big Stick.

And to my surprise, I really did not like it that much anyway.

So all that pretending had not been necessary after all.

And sometimes, without even planning to, she gave us a new word, a good laugh, and a memory that would last for years.

12

The Feather at the Window

Lynn and I were the only ones left in the classroom.

It was recess, but neither of us felt like going outside. The room was quiet, almost too quiet, with only the soft hum of the lights above us.

Mrs. Grace was not there either.

She had gone next door to the church. There was a funeral that day for Mantan Moreland, a Black actor and comedian who played the chauffeur in several Charlie Chan movies. Many of the adults were helping at the church.

Lynn leaned against the windowsill.

"Look," she whispered.

Outside, along the black wall of the church, something white kept bouncing up and down.

Only a little bit of it showed, maybe four inches, bobbing slowly as if it had a mind of its own.

Up.

Down.

Up.

Down.

We stared at it.

"What is that?" I asked.

Lynn squinted. “It looks like a feather.”

We kept watching as it floated and bounced while someone walked past the wall, completely hidden except for that one strange feather popping into view again and again.

It looked so silly that we could not help ourselves.

We started laughing.

Every time it bounced, we laughed harder.

When the bell rang, we wiped our eyes and hurried back to our seats.

Later that afternoon, Mrs. Grace returned.

Her face was soft and thoughtful, the way it got when she had been somewhere serious.

She set her purse down and said, “Children, I want you to know something special.”

We sat quietly.

“I saw Tina Turner today at the funeral,” she said.

Our heads snapped up.

“Tina Turner?” someone whispered.

Mrs. Grace nodded.

“She was wearing a beautiful hat,” she continued. “Big and elegant, with a large feather.”

Lynn and I looked at each other.

Our eyes went wide.

Then we both covered our mouths.

Because suddenly, everything made sense.

We had not seen Tina Turner.

We had not seen her face.

But we had seen her feather.

Bouncing.

Up and down.

Along the black church wall.

When the laughter finally burst out of us, Mrs. Grace raised an eyebrow.

"What is so funny?" she asked.

Lynn and I could not even explain it properly.

"We saw her," Lynn said between giggles.

"Well," Mrs. Grace said with a smile, "then I suppose you did."

And from that day on, whenever something strange floated past the window, we would whisper,

"There goes Tina Turner again."

13

By Sixth Grade, Things Were Different

A lot had changed at Glorious Baptist Day School between the time I started in second grade and the time I reached sixth grade.

When I first started school there, one of our yearly traditions happened before school even began. Every summer, my mother would take us to the teachers' bookstore with a list of books we needed for the year. Because she was a credentialed teacher, she also bought the teacher's editions, especially for the math books. She bought books for both me and my sister, and when we got back to the car, she would always complain about how much they cost. It was just part of the ritual of getting ready for school.

We only bought uniforms every other year because my mother always bought them a little big so we could grow into them.

By the time I was in sixth grade, even the uniforms had changed.

When I first started, the girls wore plaid jumpers with white blouses that had Peter Pan collars. We also wore little ribbon bows made from the same plaid fabric, and some girls had matching plaid headbands too. The boys wore dark brown corduroy-type pants with white shirts. All of us, boys and girls, wore forest green V-neck cardigans with the school crest on the left side. Back then, boys wore only slacks, and girls wore only jumpers. No girls wore pants.

Another big change was lunch.

When I started in second grade, every student brought lunch from home every day. My mother used to make my lunches. I remember getting things like Snack Packs, Twinkies, honey buns, and sometimes little boxes of raisins. Of course, there was always a sandwich too.

Thinking back, I also remember a time in second grade when I hardly ate lunch for almost a month. There was a girl named Pearl Dyson who took my lunch every day because I had good stuff in it. She was a little chubby girl, and she told me she would beat me up if I did not give it to her and that I better not tell anybody. For a while, I stayed quiet. Then one day my aunt found out and stepped in. After that, Pearl never took my lunch again. Not long after that, she left the school.

Later, things changed and we started getting hot lunches.

We would walk from the school down to the church on the corner and go into the basement, where there was a kitchen and rows of tables and chairs. Some of the tables were those picnic-style ones where you had to step over the bench to sit down. I remember the glass guard over the food, and I remember one dish the students called goulash, a word I had never heard before. At the time, I thought it just meant soup. We would get a big scoop of it with a square of cornbread. I know that cannot be the only thing we ever ate, but it is the one meal I remember most clearly.

The books changed too.

After a while, we did not have to buy books every summer anymore because the school began providing them. Each classroom had a set of books in the back, along with workbooks we could write in and keep at the end of the year. Then the next class would get a fresh set of materials. That was a big improvement.

Another change came when we got a new teacher near the end of fifth grade, someone who was either a resource specialist or a reading specialist. She worked with children who needed extra help. That was new too, and it showed that the school was growing and trying to meet more students' needs.

The class sizes changed over the years as well.

When I was in second grade, the classes were smaller. Then, as the years went on, they grew. By the time I was in sixth grade, there were eleven of us in my grade. Years earlier there had been fewer. By sixth grade, we also shared space with younger students, and the school felt fuller, busier, and more developed than it had when I first arrived.

Things changed.

Things improved.

Things evolved.

And in many ways, I grew right along with the school.

14

Performances and Activities

Sometimes all of the students would gather on the playground and sit in a U shape while visitors came to do special activities for us. Those days always felt exciting because we never knew exactly what to expect.

One time, a group from a karate school came and gave a demonstration. They showed us karate drills and broke wooden boards with their hands and feet. At the time, it seemed amazing. Looking back, it was probably also a way to advertise their karate school and get children interested in joining. It did not work on me, but I do not know whether some of the other students went home asking to sign up.

Another time, a man came who was the father of someone from Gun Smoke, though I cannot remember his name now. He spoke to the children and took pictures with us. Back then, that felt like a very big deal.

We also had Marc Copage who played Corey on the show Julia, come and speak to us. That time, instead of meeting on the playground, we gathered in the church. I remember that making the whole event feel even more important.

Not all of our activities happened at school.

I remember one especially big trip that was advertised not only to us as students, but also to the larger community. It was a trip to Big Bear. It took place on a day when there was no school, and we had to arrive very early in the morning to get on the bus. We were told to dress warmly.

Everybody was excited.

The children talked about the snow all the way there. For many of us, it was a big deal to be going somewhere where we would actually see snow. There was so much chatter and anticipation on the bus. Everybody seemed happy and eager for the adventure ahead.

I was excited too, at least at first.

But as soon as I stepped off the bus in Big Bear, the very first thing that happened was that I got hit hard in the face with a snowball. It must have been packed very tightly because when it hit me, it did not just fall apart. It felt solid.

Then, after being hit in the face, I slipped in the snow and fell on my bottom.

From that point on, I was miserable.

I did not enjoy anything else about that trip. After being hit in the face with a snowball and then falling in the snow, the only thing I really remember is how cold my toes were for the rest of the day. Very, very cold.

Meanwhile, everyone else kept talking about how much fun they had. They talked about the snow all the way back on the bus too, replaying the day and laughing about it.

But I was not impressed anymore.

From that day forward, I decided that I did not like Big Bear.

And I did not like snow.

15

Students Came and Went

One thing about Glorious Baptist Day School was that not every student stayed for a long time.

Some children came for only a short season. They were there just long enough to leave an impression, and then they were gone.

One time, we had a little girl whose mother was an airline stewardess. When she enrolled her daughter in the school, she already knew they would not be there very long. I think the little girl stayed only two or three weeks. But in that short time, she left a mark on me. She was an amazing artist. I had never seen a child draw so well. She actually taught me how to draw a few things, and I remembered those lessons and used them later on. She was petite, with a very pleasant personality, and she was in fifth grade while I was in sixth.

Another time, we had a child from Africa. He spoke with an African accent that sounded very proper, distinct, and matter-of-fact, almost as if he naturally spoke with authority. I do not remember how long he stayed, but it was not more than about a month. One thing I do remember clearly was how he corrected the rest of us whenever we said "kids." He would say, "A kid is a goat. We are children." That stayed with me. I do not remember why he came or why he left, but I remember him.

There were other temporary students too.

Sometimes a regular student would bring a cousin who was staying with the family for a little while, and that child would attend school with us for a short time. Then there were students like Juanita, who might come one year, not come the next, and then return later. We eventually learned that in her family's case, they had moved away for her father's job. When that work was finished, they came back to the area, returned to their regular house, and she resumed school at Glorious.

That happened more than once with different students.

Some children were only passing through.

Others left and came back.

The teachers changed some too, though not as much as the students.

Most of the teachers stayed the same while I was there, but for some reason, fourth grade seemed to change a lot. I do not really know why, but I remember there being three or four different teachers in fourth grade during my years at the school. Fifth and sixth grade were almost always a combination class because there were never enough students to fill a whole class for either grade by itself. At one point, third and fourth grade were combined too.

Looking back, I think many parents wanted their children to get a basic foundation first. Once the children finished second or third grade, some families moved them into public school, or at least into a different school. Glorious was a place where children could get started, get grounded, and then sometimes move on.

That was simply part of the life of the school.

People came.

People left.

Some returned.

And even when they were only with us for a short while, they still became part of the story.

16

Discipline Back Then

Back then, corporal punishment was still a part of school life. Children could get spanked on the hand or on the behind for behavior that was considered unacceptable. At the time, that was normal. It was simply one of the ways schools handled discipline, and most of us accepted it as part of life without questioning it very much.

One time, I did something that was considered very bad, though at the moment I did it, I did not fully understand how wrong it was.

A few of us sixth graders had gone into the fourth-grade classroom for some reason. While we were there, I noticed that a word on the board was misspelled. It was supposed to say quiet, but it was written incorrectly. Without thinking, I blurted out, "Wow, I did not know teachers could be dumb."

I think I was mostly reacting to the misspelled word and thinking out loud, but that did not make it any better.

The teacher did not hear me at the time, and nobody said anything right then. But apparently one or two of the girls who were with me did tell, because before long, Mrs. Grace called me in to talk, along with the other girls who had been there.

After that, we had to go back and apologize.

I think all of us got told on, even though I was the one who had made the comment. I was not deeply apologetic at first, not because I wanted to hurt anyone, but because I had not meant it the way it sounded. I had simply noticed the mistake and said the first thing that came to mind. But Mrs. Grace explained to me that the problem was not just what I noticed. It was the way I handled it.

She told me there was a respectful way to let a teacher know that something was misspelled without doing it publicly or in a way that caused embarrassment.

That lesson stayed with me.

I was a child, and children do childish things. But that time, I learned that being right about something does not give you the right to be rude about it.

I did not get a spanking for that incident.

Another time, though, I did.

And what is interesting is that this time, I got in trouble not for saying something, but for saying nothing.

Some of the boys had come up with a disgusting trick. They put a mirror on a shoe and positioned it so they could look up under the girls' skirts. The boys were sixth graders, and they were trying to look under the skirts of the fifth-grade girls. At some point, Mrs. Grace found out what was happening, and she was furious.

She called the girls together and asked us about it.

She wanted to know whether we knew what the boys were doing.

As far as I remember, the sixth-grade girls had not said anything. Maybe one of the younger girls tipped her off. I do not know. I only know that once she found out, everybody was dealt with.

The boys got spanked for what they had done.

And we girls got spanked for not telling.

That was the logic back then.

The adults expected us to speak up, and if we did not, we could be punished too.

Looking back now, it is striking how differently things were handled in those days. I do not remember the school calling home to explain what had happened. They did not seem to feel the need to involve parents in every disciplinary matter. They simply handled it themselves, right there at school, and that was that.

Years later, after we had all become adults, I spoke with one of the girls who had been spanked in sixth grade over that incident. She told me she had been traumatized by it because her parents had never spanked her before. That had been the very first time she had ever been hit as punishment.

It is amazing how an incident like that can affect someone forever.

That child grew up to become an advocate against child abuse.

Looking back now, I understand even more clearly that what adults once called discipline could leave wounds that lasted far beyond childhood. What seemed normal at the time was not always harmless, and the impact of those moments could follow a person for years.

17

Imaginary Trip in an Airplane

One day, the whole school was told that we were in for a surprise.

We were taken over to the church, where a large screen had been set up over the pulpit as if we were about to watch a movie. The entire school walked over together and sat down in the cushioned chairs, the kind where you pulled the seat down before sitting. They felt soft and comfortable, and the whole thing already seemed different from an ordinary school day.

Then the program began.

It started as if we were in the cockpit of an airplane. They showed people sitting on a plane, and we were told to imagine that we were taking a trip ourselves. We were supposed to close our eyes and picture ourselves flying. Before long, we had arrived in Africa.

At least, that was how it felt.

They showed us different places, different people, and different scenes, and they talked us through the experience so that it felt like we had actually traveled there. For children like us, it was exciting. It was not just a lesson. It felt like an adventure.

After the imaginary trip was over, a group of Nigerian men was introduced to us.

As I understood it, they had come over on work visas, and they were going to be working at the school. One was a bus driver. One was a custodian. And one of them became the principal, Mr. Bota.

I remember him especially well.

He used to tell me that I looked like a little Nigerian girl. At the time, I did not fully understand all that he meant, but I remembered it because he said it with such warmth and certainty. Then, on the day I graduated from sixth grade, I took a picture with him and his wife. They told me that if they had a daughter, she would probably look like me.

That stayed with me.

What began as an imaginary airplane trip to Africa somehow became something more personal. It was not just about seeing pictures on a screen or pretending to travel somewhere far away. It was also about meeting real people, hearing their voices, and feeling a connection to a place that had been presented to us as distant and unfamiliar.

For a moment, Africa did not feel so far away.

It felt close enough to imagine.

And close enough to recognize something of myself in it.

18

Talia

Talia had been in our class for as long as I could remember. When I entered second grade, she was already there, and by sixth grade she was still part of our little group. She was one of those classmates who seemed woven into the fabric of the school year after year.

I remember that at one point Talia had a very bad car accident. She was out of school for a few months. When she finally came back, something had changed. She had become the best reader in the class, and she read incredibly fast. I do not know whether being away from school had anything to do with it, but when she returned, she seemed stronger in that area than anyone else.

Talia was a petite girl with a light yellow complexion and jet-black wavy hair. She was not the kind of girl who spent recess standing around talking. She liked action. Every chance she got, she played with the younger boys. She would chase them around and play army with them. I guess you could say she was a tomboy. Even though she wore her school uniform skirt, she often had on shoes that looked like combat boots, and somehow that suited her perfectly.

She spent almost every recess marching the younger boys around the playground in a single file line. That was what she really enjoyed doing.

She was being raised by a single mom, and as far as I knew, she did not have any siblings.

19

The Youngest in the Class

I was the youngest student in our group of eleven.

I was not the smallest, but I had the latest birthday. My birthday was November 21, and the birthday before mine was November 1. That meant every year I was the last one to turn the age everyone else had already reached. I always noticed things like that.

Kiki, on the other hand, was the smallest one in the class. She was petite, with a yellow complexion, and everybody called her by her nickname. Her real name was beautiful and unusual, and it had ten letters. I remember one time in second grade when we had a substitute teacher. She looked at Kiki and said, "Your name is beautiful. It is bigger than you are."

That made us laugh.

Her name became a challenge for the class because it had so many letters. The children used to take turns trying to spell it. It was one of those little things that made Kiki stand out. She was also younger than a lot of people realized. Her aunt, Ro Ro, was in our class too, and even though they were both born in the same year, Ro Ro was five months older than Kiki.

Kiki and I spent a lot of time together in third grade.

At one point, I think we were best friends.

I remember one day when the two of us went into our third-grade teacher's classroom and sang a song to her. We stood in front of the teacher holding hands and sang a song that we had made up ourselves. It went like this:

We are the two, we are the two.
We are the two-two.
We are the two, we are the two.
We are the two-two-two.

That was our song.

Only the two of us sang it because it was only about us.

The day we sang it to the teacher, none of the other students were in the room. Everyone else was outside at recess. It was just Kiki, me, and the teacher. I do not remember whether we had practiced it first or just made it up and decided to perform it on the spot, but I do remember how special it felt to us. We were proud of our little song, and in that moment, it seemed important enough to present.

That was the kind of friendship children can have, simple and sweet, full of little private meanings that matter deeply at the time.

Even now, I smile when I think about it.

I was the youngest in the class.

Kiki was the smallest.

And for a while, the two of us were simply "the two."

20

The Spelling Bee

A few weeks before the spelling bee, Mrs. Lewis asked me to spell the word scout, as in Girl Scout.

I could not do it.

She looked at me with confusion all over her face.

"Your last name is Scott," she said. "You should not have any trouble spelling scout. It is only one letter different."

I wanted to explain.

I did not spell by sounding words out.

I could only spell words I had memorized.

If I had not seen a word before, the letters did not just arrange themselves in my mind.

But I did not yet have the words to explain that.

So I just stared at my paper.

The day of the spelling bee started differently from most school days.

That morning, my mother handed me a one-hundred-dollar bill.

"Take this to the office," she said. "It is for your tuition."

She had never done that before.

I folded the bill carefully and slipped it into my shoe so I would not lose it. I could feel it under my foot every time I walked. Somehow, it made me feel important.

That day, the school held a spelling bee for the third, fourth, fifth, and sixth grades together.

I was not a great speller.

Everybody knew that, including me.

My sister made it to the second or third round before she got the word exercise. She spelled it with a z instead of an s, and she had to sit down.

I kept standing.

Round after round.

When it came down to just a few of us, the student in front of me missed her word.

Then it was my turn.

"Your word is," the teacher said, "appreciate."

I froze.

I did not know how to spell it.

Not really.

I just started saying letters.

"A-P-P-R-E-C-I-A-T-E."

"Correct," the judge said.

My eyes widened.

The final word was appropriate.

My heart beat so hard I could hear it in my ears.

Again, I did not know exactly how I knew it, but somehow I spelled it right.

When the bell rang, I had won.

I stared at the floor.

I think that hundred-dollar bill in my shoe was my lucky charm.

Looking back, I think the plan may have been to send the winner on to a regional spelling bee. But it never went any further.

Probably because even the teachers knew my win was more luck than skill.

Still, I had won.

And all I really knew was that sometimes I surprised everyone, including myself.

21

The Girls in My Class

By sixth grade, our class of eleven had become a very familiar group. We all knew one another well by then, and each person had her own look, personality, and place in the class.

Since Talia already has her own chapter, I will start with Monique.

Monique was the classmate who looked the most like me. She and I were very close in skin tone, hairline, and height, although I was a little taller and a little thicker. She was born in July. We both had sisters in fourth grade, which gave us something else in common.

One day after lunch, Monique asked me for my telephone number. I did not understand why she needed it, because she had called me before. I told her I would give it to her later, but she insisted that I tell it to her right then, so I did. I said the numbers slowly: 2-3-2-4-4-1-2.

That night, I got a call from Ray.

The moment I heard his voice, I knew exactly what had happened. Monique had asked for my number so Ray could write it down. I felt betrayed. It was such a small thing, but at that age it felt big. I had trusted that she was asking for herself, and instead she had asked for someone else. Childhood friendships could be sweet, but they could also sting in small and surprising ways.

By then, several of Monique's relatives had also begun attending Glorious. Their family had a pattern with names. They all started with the letter M. There was her boy cousin Mitchell, who was a year older than she was. Then came Monique, her girl cousin Marisa, her sister Monet, and her little cousin Miranda. They were all different ages, like steps in a family line. Monique and Monet were dark-skinned like me, while the three cousins were lighter, more of a medium light brown complexion.

Then there was Kiki, whom I already discussed. She was much more outgoing than some of the other girls and carried herself with a kind of spark.

RoRo was Kiki's aunt, which always seemed interesting to us since the two of them were in the same class and best friends. They had both been born in the same year, but RoRo was about five months older than Kiki. RoRo was much taller than Kiki. She was tall and thin, caramel-colored, with medium-length hair and glasses. She had a quiet, shy way about her that was very different from Kiki's more outgoing personality.

Then there was Lynn.

Lynn was the tallest girl in the class. She was also caramel-colored and wore glasses, but she did not look anything like RoRo. She had medium-length hair and a strong presence about her.

Lynn often seemed to know more than the rest of us about things outside our little school world. One Monday, she came to school with a Jackson 5 program. She had gone over the weekend to a Michael Jackson concert, and the program was beautiful, full of colorful pictures of the Jackson 5. We all gathered around to look at it.

Lynn told us she had gone to the Forum, but we did not understand what she meant. None of us had any real knowledge of the

Los Angeles Forum, where celebrities performed. We thought she was saying she had gone to a farm. An actual farm. We could not figure out why the Jackson 5 would be at a farm with animals. Looking back, it is funny, but at the time we were completely serious. We were trying to make sense of what she said with the little bit of knowledge we had. Once we finally understood, it all seemed even more exciting. Lynn had not gone somewhere ordinary. She had gone somewhere big, glamorous, and far beyond anything most of us knew.

My funniest memory of Lynn, though, went all the way back to second grade. Our teacher was telling the class different things to bring for a party we were about to have. She told Lynn to bring sandwich spread. She repeated it several times and even asked Lynn whether she understood. Lynn said yes. I was only seven years old, but somehow I knew Lynn did not understand what sandwich spread was. Sure enough, she showed up the next day with sandwich bread. The teacher ended up having to leave and go to the store to buy the sandwich spread herself. That memory still makes me laugh.

When she was younger, she had sat on a furnace or something hot and had a permanent mark on the back of her thigh. It was darker than the rest of her skin.

Lynn had a brother named Tyree, and he spent a lot of time teasing me and calling me names. He always called me Black as if it were supposed to bother me. Little did he know, I did not have a problem with being called Black. My aunt had taught me that Black was beautiful and that I was beautiful.

One time, Tyree threw my ring up onto the roof. It had been my favorite Christmas gift that year. The adults made him go up on the roof and look for it, but he said he could not find it. After that, I never saw that ring again. I never really understood why he disliked me so much. Looking back, I sometimes wonder whether he may have been self-conscious himself. He was dark-skinned too, darker than I was, and perhaps he had been teased about it by lighter people in his own family. I do not know for sure. That is only my guess. What I do know is that I loved that ring, and once he took it from me, it was gone forever.

Then there was Juanita, steady and familiar, part of the class rhythm by sixth grade.

And then there was me, Denise, right there among all of those different girls, trying to find my own place in the group.

That was our circle of girls.

Seven of us in all.

Different shades, different heights, different personalities, different family stories.

And together, we made up the girls of sixth grade at Glorious Baptist Day School.

22

The Boys in My Class

The boys in the class were all like brothers to me.

I never liked any of them as a boyfriend, but I loved them all like brothers. They were the brothers I never had. I was cool with all of them, and they were all cool with me.

There were only four boys in our sixth-grade class, but each of them had a distinct personality and presence.

First there was Ray.

Ray was light-skinned, with jet-black hair that was always neatly cut. I always liked seeing boys with a fresh, neat haircut, and Ray always looked well put together. He was the youngest child in his family and had older siblings who were almost grown. His mother helped the teacher whenever she was able, so he came from one of those families that seemed closely connected to the life of the school.

Then there was Donnell.

Donnell was the cool boy. He was a thin, brown-skinned boy who wore his hair in a blowout, which made his Afro look even bigger than it normally would have. Looking back, he reminds me of Todd Bridges from Diff'rent Strokes, although of course we did not know about that at the time. Donnell always wore the latest shoes.

He was the first one to wear high-top Converse All Stars, and that alone made him stand out.

Many of us in sixth grade had siblings in the fourth grade, including Monique, Juanita, Anthony, and me. But Donnell's little brother David was in the third grade. Donnell had personality too. He was the one who could say something unexpected and have the whole class laughing.

Then there was Anthony.

Anthony's complexion reminded me of my grandfather's coffee. My grandfather used to put a lot of cream in his coffee, and that was the color Anthony was to me, coffee with a lot of cream. He had a low Afro and a nice look about him. All the girls liked Anthony. He also had a little sister in my sister's class named Annette, and Annette was my sister Yvette's best friend.

Then there was Louis.

Louis was the tallest and biggest boy in the class. He looked older than he actually was, almost as if he could have passed for being a few years ahead of us. Even so, he had a pleasant smile and was always helpful to adults. Some people would probably have called him a gentle giant. His father was a policeman, and Louis had already decided that he wanted to become a policeman too when he grew up. I think he was an only child.

That was our group of boys.

Just four of them.

But with Ray's neatness, Donnell's humor, Anthony's good looks, and Louis's size and helpfulness, they added their own energy to the class.

Together with the seven girls, they completed our class of eleven.

A small class.

A memorable class.

And by sixth grade, we all knew each other well enough to feel like our own little world.

23

Graduation Day

The air was busy that morning.

It was graduation day.

We arrived at school all dressed up and ready. Soon we put on our white caps and gowns to prepare for the walk over to the church. We had already seen one another in them a few days earlier when we took our individual graduation pictures. Most people probably did not notice, but if you looked very closely at my picture, you could see that I had a busted lip. That morning, I had been playing with my little cousin Andre, and while we were fooling around, he accidentally bumped me in the mouth with his head. It hurt much worse than it looked. My aunt put some Vaseline on it and said I would be all right.

It was a special day.

When I graduated from sixth grade, my mother gave me a silver heart-shaped locket. Years later, I gave that same locket to my oldest daughter when she graduated from sixth grade. I had hoped it would become a family tradition. But when my granddaughter reached sixth grade, I asked my daughter whether she still had it, and she said probably not. She told me she had not really started keeping things until she was over sixteen. And just like that, the tradition was lost.

Our caps and gowns were made of a heavy, broadcloth-like material, and they were very, very white. We had been instructed not to eat or do anything that might get them dirty once we put them on. When it was time to go, we walked from the school to the church in height order.

That meant Kiki was first in the girls' line, and Lynn was at the back because she was the tallest. Juanita stood in front of Lynn, and I stood in front of Juanita. RoRo was in front of me. At the front of the girls' line were Kiki, then Talia, then Monique. The boys' line was simpler because there were only four of them: Ray, Darrell, Anthony, and Louis.

I was first on the program because I had to give the welcome speech.

We also had several other performances, including our class song, which we all sang together. Mrs. Grace had changed the words to make them fit our graduation, but everyone already knew the tune because it was a popular song at the time. Our parents, relatives, and friends applauded all of our performances.

Then it was time for the awards.

One by one, names were called, and students walked to the podium to receive their certificates. There were awards for things like most improved, best in math, and most creative. Then came the one I received:

Most Conscientious.

I smiled and walked slowly up to the podium to get my award while the audience applauded loudly. The truth is, I had no idea what I was being honored for because I did not know what conscientious meant. Still, I assumed it had to be something good. Why would anyone get an award for something bad? Besides, I already knew that I was a good student and a good person. I tried hard to do the right thing.

The first person I asked about the meaning was my mother. The second thing I did was look it up in the dictionary, probably at her direction. My mother was a teacher, and one of her favorite things to say when I asked about a word was, "Look it up in the dictionary."

I used to think that made no sense sometimes, especially when I was asking how to spell a word. I would wonder, How can I look it up in the dictionary if I do not know how to spell it? Still, somehow, I usually found the word I was looking for.

One of my favorite possessions back then was a small pocket dictionary that I kept in my purse. There were so many words I did not know, and I used that little dictionary often.

Anyway, I came to understand that conscientious meant having a conscience and being careful to do the right thing.

That sounded like me.

Our class of eleven was the largest sixth-grade class to graduate during all the years I had been at Glorious. When I first arrived in second grade, the school only went up to third grade, and then another grade was added each year. The year before us, there had been six graduates. The year before that, there had been only two.

Whenever the sixth-grade graduation was held, the kindergarten graduation took place at the same time. That was one way the school made the event feel full and festive. The kindergarten class usually had between fifteen and twenty students, so they helped fill the church with proud families and excited visitors. The kindergartners graduated first, and then the sixth graders followed.

It was a nice program.

Everyone was excited.

The kindergartners were dressed in white too, and the whole day felt bright, formal, and important. By then, I knew I was leaving behind something special. Glorious Baptist Day School had shaped so much of my childhood, and now I was standing at the end of it in a white cap and gown, giving speeches, singing songs, and receiving an award for a word I had to go look up later.

That was graduation day.

And whether I fully understood it then or not, I was walking out of one chapter of life and into another.

24

What Glorious Gave Me

When I look back on my years at Glorious Baptist Day School, I do not just remember lessons, classrooms, uniforms, or performances.

I remember being shaped.

Glorious gave me more than an education. It gave me memories that stayed with me, lessons that reached far beyond childhood, and people whose voices I can still hear all these years later.

It was there that I learned how to speak up, and also when to be quiet.

It was there that I learned that leadership did not always have to be loud.

It was there that I learned responsibility, friendship, courage, and how to carry myself in the world.

At Glorious, we learned in ways that were both ordinary and unforgettable. We learned from books and spelling bees, from songs and speeches, from laughter and correction, from teachers who expected something of us, and from classmates who became part of the story of who we were.

Some lessons were small at the time but turned out to be lasting. A French song. A crochet needle. A vocabulary word. A moment of being trusted to help younger children. A teacher's words spoken at just the right time. All of it mattered.

Even the things I did not fully understand then became part of me later.

That school was not perfect.

But it was powerful.

It gave me a foundation.

It gave me stories.

And it gave me a sense that I was part of something meaningful.

When I was a little girl at Glorious, I said that one day I would do something great.

I did not know then what that would look like.

I only knew that deep down, I believed it.

Now, when I look back, I can see that Glorious was one of the places where that belief was planted and watered.

It was one chapter of my life.

But it was a glorious one.

Years have passed since our days at Glorious Baptist Day School, and life carried each of us in different directions. When we were children, we could not have imagined all the roads our lives would take. Yet in many ways, the seeds of who we would become were already there.

Ray now works in administration for a water company in Riverside, California.

Darrell, peace be upon him, was murdered in his twenties. His life was cut short far too soon, and his memory remains with us.

Anthony owns and operates his own plumbing company.

Lewis fulfilled the dream he had even as a child. He worked as a police officer, following in his father's footsteps. Now he serves as a city councilman in the city where he lives.

KiKi is a software engineer and resides in Los Angeles.

RoRo and Lynn are both social worker and reside in Los Angeles.

Talia lives in Texas.

Monique is a real estate broker, the owner of several properties and restaurants, and she resides in Texas.

Juanita is a Superior Court judge in Los Angeles.

And then there is Denise.

Denise became the mother of eleven children and has written eleven books, including this one. She is a college professor, a business owner, and a school board candidate. Even as a child, she always believed that one day she would do something great.

And she has.